BELLA
and the
MASTER CRAFTSMAN

Written by

Aryanna Bax Liddell

Illustrated by

Zhiying Chen

WestBow Press books may be ordered through booksellers or by contacting:

WestBow Press
A Division of Thomas Nelson & Zondervan
1663 Liberty Drive
Bloomington, IN 47403
www.westbowpress.com
844-714-3454

ISBN: 978-1-6642-8106-6 (sc)
ISBN: 978-1-6642-8108-0 (hc)
ISBN: 978-1-6642-8107-3 (e)

Library of Congress Control Number: 2022919113

Print information available on the last page.

WestBow Press rev. date: 10/17/2022

WESTBOW
PRESS®
A DIVISION OF THOMAS NELSON
& ZONDERVAN

For Daniel, Annabella, and Emilia, and for my mother
who first encouraged me to write stories.
-A.B.L.

"Cock-a-doodle-doo!" The rooster crowed at 6:42
and morning began to dawn.
Inside Bella stirs, covered her ears,
clutched the covers, and let out a yawn.
But before she dozed back to dreams on horseback,
the sun shone upon her eyes.
And squinting and turning, she greeted the morning
with a groan at the orange sunrise.

Later that day, she went out to play
until it started to rain.
She ran through the mud, and fell down with a 'thud'.
Her clothes now dirty and stained.
She went back inside, her enthusiasm died.
She cried, and pouted, and whined,
"How can the first day of summer be such a bummer?
Why is God so unkind?"

Her father was in the kitchen when he heard her sniffling,
and her cries tugged at his heartstrings.
He got her a clean shirt, and some delicious dessert:
some fruit and strawberry pudding.
But she remained still upon the window sill,
mad, grumpy, and drenched.
Eyebrows knit together, she frowned at the weather
"Dad, it's a summer's day misspent!"

"Today was supposed to be fun but now that is all gone
because the rain came out of nowhere.
Now I can't play outside and I'm dissatisfied.
Does God not see or care?"

"Is the rain so bad that it would make you this sad?"
Her dad wiped away her tears.
"Look again and tell me, what do you see?"
And there she saw a rainbow appear.
Bella gasped and pressed her face on the glass.
Suddenly she was no longer brooding.
What can cause such a shift but only a rare gift—
that of rain clouds and sun rays fusing.

"Bella, there is a reason God gave us the seasons,
that's to show us His skill and love.
Forests, rivers, and mountains, aren't they abounding
with His affection from above?
God spent the time making everything sublime
with different colors and shades.
He designed the flowers, divined the rain showers
and the dew on every grass blade.
The bugs, the stones, the waves, the glaciers, and the caves,
from stars above to the deepest sea,
even barnacles to the smallest particles—
all creation reveals His majesty!"

Bella listened and sat there, still drying her hair,
marveling at what her dad said,
"Now I see things that seem bad, have beauty to them, dad."
Her father nodded his head.
As the sky held its glory, her dad recalled the story
of the promise told long ago,
"Remember the flood and the ark, and earth days so dark,
and of a love sealed with a rainbow?
There up in the sky, that rainbow cast high
only gives a taste of His creativity;
but even more so it's another way to show
His beautiful grace and mercy.

"We have a craftsman so dedicated to the world He created
and to the people who dwelt on earth.
Though we are sinners, He made a plan to deliver
And offered a chance for rebirth."

"So even when I mumbled and even when I grumbled
God could still forgive me?"
Bella exclaimed because she was ashamed.
But dad said, "Yes, certainly.
Because our awesome Creator had a plan much greater—
one that will set us all free:
Jesus Christ, His Son, came to die for everyone,
to save you and me.
That was a very sad day, but it was the only way
for God to restore us to Him.

Now we don't need to mope, for he rose again to give hope
that our God will ultimately win.
And through the ages, even creation praises
the fulfillment of God's promise.
Now creation yearns for Jesus' return
and a world free from darkness.

"Dad, I'm so blind, and so unkind,"
Bella was sorry for her behavior.
"In my greed, now I see my need
for Jesus to be my savior."
The skies cleared, and the sun reappeared
and her dad drew her in for an embrace,
"We are all offenders, so we must always remember
God's wonderful, beautiful grace."

When the day ended, and the sun descended,
Bella ran out to meet its rays.
The sky like fire, and the crickets form the choir,
She cries, "The world is a glimpse of God's face!
How can one grumble at rain, or call the trees plain,
or not be thankful for fresh air?
When everywhere you look, every cranny, every nook,
our God's handiwork is there.
From when the universe began to his master plan,
our world is full of His artistry.
He creates masterpieces, and gave us His Son Jesus,
To tell us his plan and story."
Bella was humbled, and she no longer grumbled
about days sunny or rainy.
Awestruck and captivated, she eagerly waited
For the day God will display His full glory.

A Note from the Author:

Bella and the Master Craftsman is inspired from an article I had written years ago when I was in Singapore working with a team on a UNEP position paper on Environmental Law. The reality of the effects of sin on God's creation became very tangible then. But there is hope.

Colossians 1:23 says the gospel is proclaimed in all creation (ESV). It all points back to Jesus. Jesus, the Son of God, magnificent, brilliant and perfect, came down to earth to die on the cross to pay the price for the sins of man. He rose again after three days and someday He will return to judge the earth, restore His elect to Him, and make a new heaven and a new earth. It is a Love surpassing knowledge that He has bestowed upon us. When we receive Him as Lord and Savior, we will live in His embrace with His beauty and glory for all eternity. It is the most remarkable story of the ages.

My hope is when you look out, you'll see His divine artwork. Every minute illustration of His affection is a glimpse of the gospel and the promise awaiting us—all across the earth is a unique display of the Master Craftsman, our Creator, and Mankind's Savior.

O Lord, our Lord,
    how majestic is your name in all the earth!
You have set your glory above the heavens.
When I look at your heavens, the work of your fingers,
    the moon and the stars, which you have set in place,
what is man that you are mindful of him,
    and the son of man that you care for him?
Psalm 8:1, 3-4

To whom then will you compare me,
    that I should be like him? says the Holy One.
Lift up your eyes on high and see:
    who created these?
He who brings out their host by number,
    calling them all by name;
by the greatness of his might
    and because he is strong in power,
    not one is missing.

Why do you say, O Jacob,
    and speak, O Israel,
"My way is hidden from the Lord,
    and my right is disregarded by my God"?
Have you not known? Have you not heard?
The Lord is the everlasting God,
    the Creator of the ends of the earth.
He does not faint or grow weary;
    his understanding is unsearchable.
Isaiah 40:25-28

Aryanna Bax Liddell

Aryanna grew up in the Philippines where it rains an average of 144 days a year! She has a graduate degree in diplomacy and international conflict management and loves traveling God's world with her husband and two daughters. She now spends her days homeschooling her children and making stories for them from their home in (also) rainy Oregon.

Zhiying Chen

Zhiying is an illustrator based in New York State. She graduated from Maryland Institute College of Art, BFA illustration program; Syracuse University, MFA illustration program. Check out her work at www.zhiyingc.com.

Printed in the United States
by Baker & Taylor Publisher Services